The Encounter

The Encounter
Copyright © 2021 by Tim Tweedie

Credits

Cover art & illustrations © Tim Tweedie

ISBN: 978-1-945539-45-9

The Encounter

Tim Tweedie

Dunecrest Press

Contents

Chapter One

Something Special

"Welcome to Yosemite!" said the young forest ranger as I pulled out my annual National Parks Pass and waved it at her.

"Would you like a map and park newsletter so you know what's going on this summer?" she continued.

"No thanks, Cindy," I returned after a quick look at her name tag. "I would like to know the park weather forecast for the next few days."

"Well, are you going into the valley or up towards Tuolumne Meadows?" she merrily replied.

"I'm going to continue up Highway 120 through the meadows then down to Lee Vining. I plan to hike and fish the Tioga Pass area over the next three days," I responded.

"Then you're in luck! Temperatures will be in the high 70's Monday through Friday with the usual cool nights, just above freezing, and a slight chance of a few thunder clouds in the late afternoons."

"Pretty much what I'd hoped for. I appreciate your help. Have a good one," I replied as I stepped on the gas and slowly made my way into the park.

Yosemite was my favorite National Park.

Fortunately for me, I lived just down the hill in Modesto, about a two-hour drive to the northwest park entrance above Groveland. I try to visit at least twice a year, a few days in the summer for hiking and fishing and a couple in the valley in the spring to catch the many falls that cascade down the shear cliffs.

This time I was here alone. My brother would usually fly in from Hawaii for a few days so we could hike and fish Yosemite and the eastern Sierras together. However, I received his call two days ago that something had come up that made it impossible for him to join me. I knew it must have been something important because he was as attached to these mountains as I was.

Fifteen minutes after leaving the entrance gate, I arrived at the Crane Flat store and junction where 120 made a sharp left turn to the east. About a ten mile stretch of Highway 120 continued down to join Highway 140 in Yosemite Valley.

I made the sharp left and quickly checked my gas gauge. There were no stations until Tuolumne Meadows which is about an hour's drive up the hill. I still had three-quarters of a tank, plenty to get me to Lee Vining.

I was glad I had decided to come. I had lined out almost a week on the calendar at the travel agency I owned in Modesto. Business had been strong but I still needed to get away. I knew Larry, my business manager, would take care of the office and oversee the other agents.

The drive up through the high country is incredible, one beautiful view after another. Forests of pines and firs, wide open vistas across valleys and massive granite domes, all decorate the landscape. Pullouts like the ones near Porcupine flat and Olmsted Point are a photographer's dream.

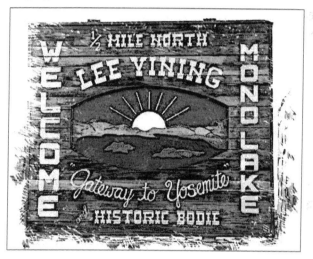

The town of Lee Vining and Mono Lake.

Then there is the beauty of Tenaya Lake, Tuolumne Meadows, Tioga Pass, and the dramatic Lee Vining Canyon where the road drops down over 3000 feet in less than ten miles to the town of Lee Vining and Mono Lake.

I pulled into the Murphey's Motel just after noon.

As I walked up to the registration counter, Betty greeted me with a warm smile.

"Good to see you again, Vince. How was the drive up?"

"As always, great. How've you and Bill been?" I inquired.

Betty and her husband, Bill, had managed the motel for years. They were friendly and outgoing people who knew everyone in town and just about everything that happened in and around Lee Vining.

"Fine! It's been a busy summer, especially since the pass opened early June, and the weather's been cooperative," she replied. "I'm glad to see you back! Where's your brother? I thought he was coming too."

"Something came up at the last minute so I'm soloing for a few days."

"That's too bad!" she responded disappointedly.

She knew how much he liked the area.

"Remember, I'm only here for tonight this time. I managed to reserve a tent cabin up at Tuolumne Meadows Lodge for a couple of nights."

"Well your room is ready," she smiled as she handed me the keys to Room 23.

I always asked for 23, but I didn't need to. Betty knew it's the one I prefer. It was on the second floor, just a few feet off Highway 395, noisy at night when the trucks ran through, but large and open, with two queen beds and the best view.

"Nicely's Restaurant and Barbecue still serving

4

good food?" I asked, knowing perfectly well that it's the only major restaurant in town and hadn't changed since before Nixon was president.

"It's either there, Snow White's across the street, or the Mobil Station up the hill," she reported. "All depends on what your stomach can take."

"Then Nicely's Barbecue it is!" I said, smiling as I licked my lips.

I took my bags to the room and headed up the block to the restaurant with my rather empty stomach leading the way.

I took a table on the outside patio.

I took a rail table on the outside patio. From there I could overlook the sidewalk and watch any interesting traffic or pedestrians who might go by. Only a few other customers were scattered around the tables.

I quickly ordered a cheeseburger and side salad and was glad to see they sold Guinness Harp Lager. After having some Harp on tap at an Irish Pub in Squaw Valley last summer, it had temporarily become my favorite Lager.

I put my hand around the cool bottle the moment it touched the table and took my first long drink. With that, I sat back to get my bearings.

The waitress was young, probably a recent graduate from the local high school. She was pleasant, slightly overweight, and had the rather annoying habit of calling everyone "Hun".

Fortunately, her eagerness to please made me quickly forgive her.

An older couple was at a table to my far left, and a middle-aged man in riding leathers with a red- checked bandanna wrapped around his head sat across the patio from me and held a large sparerib to his mouth. I guessed the Harley near the curb about fifty feet away was his.

At the table in front of me sat a lady, probably in her early thirties, wearing fitted jeans, a light blue collared blouse, and some low cut brown hiking shoes. She sat at a angle to me but I could make out the delicate features of her profile. Her hair was light brown with blond streaks. Her skin was lightly tanned and the nails on her hands were manicured. I don't think she was here to do a lot of backcountry hiking.

Just as I was taking another sip of Harp, she turned

towards me and smiled, not a broad smile, but an inquisitive and sort of sad smile.

"How are you doing? Are you just traveling through?" I asked trying not to appear too bold.

"Actually, I'm just killing time. I was supposed to meet someone here, but not anymore. I thought there was a chance that he might have made it anyway. That's what I thought when I first caught sight of you. Sorry."

"No, I'm sorry" I replied.

There was a long pause as her eyes dropped a bit towards the patio deck.

"By the way," I finally said, "my name's Vince."

She immediately looked up, taking another moment to evaluate what she should say next. I felt sorry for her knowing how hard it was to shift gears in the middle of being stood up.

"Oh, I'm Trisha," she said with a smile, her composure starting to return.

I continued with, "I just came up from Modesto for a few days to do some hiking and fishing. My brother from Hawaii was supposed to join me, but at the last moment he had to cancel. So in a way I seem to be in the same situation as you are."

"Then you just drove eight hours from Las Vegas in a rental car only to find out you'd been stood up?" she replied with a hint of anger, her composure obviously still a bit fractured.

"No, I probably shouldn't have told you that. I was just trying to make you feel better."

I paused for a moment, and tried another approach.

"All the way from Vegas in a rental car...I know Lee Vining is a hot location. Did you get to visit Barstow on the way?" I asked, thinking maybe humor would help.

"Well, I did get to stop at the large factory outlet stores there for an hour and bought a cute tank top, so maybe the entire trip wasn't a complete blow off," she returned with a coy expression on her face as she looked up at me.

She's quick when she wants to be. Picked up on what I was doing right away and ran with it. Maybe it did work.

"Yeah, I've also shopped there before. However, it's too far from Modesto for me to make a habit out of it," I replied with a slight laugh.

"Thanks," she said softly, "for trying to make me feel better. I've been quite angry since he called."

"Oh finally! Here comes my cheeseburger and salad. Have you ordered anything?" I queried.

"No, I've been too mad to do much of anything but fume," she returned.

"Then I guess it's time for you to get something to eat and join me, besides what else are you going to do? The stores will be long closed before you get as far as Barstow. Would you like something to drink?"

"Why not," she replied as she turned her seat around to my table.

I was right. Her features were delicate. Her face was lightly tanned and attractive, and highlighted by her light blue eyes. Even though she appeared delicate, the more we talked, the more I could see her inner strength and confidence.

With a wave of her hand Trisha got the waitress's attention.

"Yes ma'am, what can I get you?" asked the waitress.

Apparently the "hun" was saved for the men.

"I'd like the cheeseburger and salad with oil and balsamic vinegar dressing, if you have it."

"We sure do! Anything else ma'am?" the waitress asked patiently.

"And I'd like a Bud Light," Trisha returned.

"You got it," said the waitress as she quietly slipped away.

"We'd actually only been dating for about five months. When he asked me if I wanted to get out of town for a couple of days and see the eastern Sierras, I thought why not? I knew I needed a change of scenery. Vegas moves at a hectic pace, besides, I felt we needed some time to discuss our relationship. Goes to show you what I know," she stated matter-of-factly.

"Oh," I said, a little surprised at all the information.

"Just thought I'd share that with you now. I knew you probably were trying to figure out my situation and I just thought I'd help things along. Besides, I think I need to move on," she added.

"Good Idea! What do you do in Las Vegas?" I asked.

"I'm an emergency room nurse at Desert Springs

Hospital. After doing that job for the last eight years a little thing like being stood up shouldn't shake me...but it did...that's really strange. I would never have thought...well I guess the heart and mind don't always work together," she added, a cold Bud Light now in her hand.

"I know what you mean. I've traveled to most countries in the world and handled many difficult situations, but matters the heart still leave me amazed and often perplexed."

"Then you're a vagabond, an international drifter who travels the world doing good, kind of like a penniless Bill Gates?" Trisha offered with a teasing smile.

"It would be nice to have just the penny end of all the corporate checks Mr. Gates writes, but you're half right. I have a travel agency and work mostly with large businesses in handling their client, executive, and group travel to just about anywhere they need to be. I've had the business for ten years and really enjoy it 99% of the time," I offered.

By now Trisha was eagerly biting into her cheeseburger while I was finishing off my salad.

"Actually, not bad," I said as I swallowed a fork full of salad.

"Not bad at all," Trish added as a bit of ketchup appeared on her lip.

The more I talked to Trisha the more I liked her. She was quick and witty and seemed willing to talk about anything. This guy must be an idiot. I would have driven eight hours just to meet her...actually, in a way, I did.

As we were finishing, I asked, "Where are you staying?"

"Well, I have a room at the Murphey's Motel, so I guess I'll use that tonight and drive on back to Vegas in the morning," she replied as she laid her napkin on the table.

"I have a room at the Murphey's Motel."

"Then you have no plans for dinner? Would you like to join me?" I asked with as much enthusiasm as I dared. "I have reservations for two tonight at the Mono Lake Restaurant. It's above the lake about three miles north of town. The food's fantastic. Besides I can pick you up. You're probably staying just a few feet away from me since I'm also at the Murphy's Motel."

"I'd like that Vince. I enjoy talking with you. You help me forget about...Well, what time?"

"How does 6:30 sound?"

"Fine'" she replied. "It will give me time to try on that tank top I bought...and the green dress I forgot to mention. I can do a lot of shopping in an hour...By the way..."

"Yes," I asked.

"Room 12," she returned.

"See ya," I said as I handed the waitress a twenty.

"Thanks, hun," she returned as I lightly bit my lip.

Chapter Two

Mono Inn

I had about four hours before I needed to get showered and pick up Trisha. Plenty of time I thought to put my fly pole together and run across the street and down the canyon to Lee Vining Creek for a bit of fly fishing.

I cut down the scenic hiking trail at the south end of town. The trail started just below a small hydro electric plant that provided the local power. It followed the creek towards Mono Lake for a couple of miles before leading back up towards Highway 395 and the impressive Mono Lake Tufa Museum.

The water flow this time of year was heavy and swift. The steep canyon created a beautiful white ribbon of cascading water making it difficult to find swirls and pools in which to cast my fly.

I worked my way down along the trail, looking for one of the few locations where the creek actually leveled out a bit, and casted my fly. The current quickly grabbed it and pulled it down stream. It was about the same location where I caught a nice fourteen inch rainbow trout last year, but that was late summer when the flow was much less. I could quickly see that now wasn't a good time to fish this section of Lee Vining creek.

Back at the motel I showered and turned on the television catching the news and the stock market wrap up for the day. For a Tuesday, neither were very interesting.

My mind kept slipping back to Trisha. I wanted to know more about her. Where she was raised, her family, where she went to school, what she enjoyed doing, questions I hoped would be answered tonight at dinner.

At 6:35 I stood in front of Room 12 not wanting to appear too eager. I'd chosen the light blue polo shirt with a darker-blue sweater and cotton slacks, the one dressy outfit I'd brought with me.

As I started to knock, the door flew open.

"Hi Vince! I'm ready!" said Trisha enthusiastically.

I paused, as the saying goes, caught up in the moment. Her dress was a deep emerald green with a large collared V necked front. She accessorized with black mid heeled shoes, a wide black belt with a modest silver buckle, and a silver necklace and pendant that hung just below her neck. She carried a small black purse and had a light black shawl with silver threads, laid across her shoulders. Her hair was pulled back and tied but still managed to spread out and cascade down to her shoulders. She was a knockout!

"Wow! You're going to make Barstow a very popular place for the ladies to shop."

I could see Trisha's wide smile as I closed the door behind us and we headed out to my car.

"You like your Highlander?" Trisha asked as I opened the passenger side door.

"I've had it for a year, and so far it's been a great vehicle. It doesn't guzzle gas like a lot of the larger SUV's, has all-wheel drive for the mountains and snow, and is just large enough to pull my nineteen- foot Reinell inboard/outboard runabout. What more could a man ask for?"

"Well if you're asking me, I could think of a few things," she replied with that attractive coy smile on her face.

"I'm driving an Altima that I rented in Las Vegas," she continued. "My Audi four was in the shop. I'd caught a rock in my front window that went on and chipped my left rearview mirror. Oddly enough the rock came out of a large truck hauling a shipment of new slot machines for one of the casinos...yeah, what are those odds?" she said as she began to laugh.

Her laugh was infectious, so I began to laugh with her. Besides the thought of a bunch of slot machines throwing a rock out at her was amusing.

"You know Trisha, I can sit by one of those things for two hours tossing money in, but they never seem to toss anything back out at me!...You must be a lucky

15

lady."

"In some ways you might say I am."

We pulled up in front of the Mono Lake Inn and Restaurant. It sat on Highway 395 on the shore above Mono Lake.

"The family of the renowned photographer Ansel Adams owns this place. His granddaughter, Sarah, remodeled the large old house turning in it into a fine restaurant and art gallery for Ansel's work. I've spoken to her a couple of times on the phone about some of his signed books that I own, but we have yet to meet. She lives in the Bay area but spends a lot of time here," I explained as we walked to the front door.

"I do know his photography. My parents are fortunate to own several of his photographs. I really like his 'Clearing Winter Storm' taken in Yosemite Valley."

"That's one of my favorites too," I said enthusiastically as we walked down the stairs to the host's stand.

"Table for two for Frazier," I announced to the young male host.

"Sure! Vince Frazier, right?" he returned.

I took a closer look and then realized it was Paul who had served me here before.

"Paul, I hardly recognize you with your beard shaved off. Looking good! How've you been?"

"Working hard, but I get time off to hike the canyons and do some photography. I really like the eastern Sierras. They are constantly changing."

"Paul, this is my friend Trisha."

"Nice to meet you. Is this your first time at th Inn?" he asked.

"Yes, my very first, rather unexpected visit. I'm looking forward to dinner. Your restaurant comes highly recommended."

Paul smiled and nodded.

"I have your table ready right in front of the window ...and by the way, I'll be your waiter since I'm pulling double duty tonight. We seem to be short a waitress," he said shrugging.

"That's fine! Then I know we'll be getting excellent service," I added as Paul pulled out a chair for Trisha.

"Would you like to order drinks or an appetizer now?" Paul efficiently added.

"Not just yet," I answered, as I looked over at Trisha to get her approval.

She looked back and nodded.

"Then I'll leave the menus and return in a few minutes."

"This really is a beautiful spot. We'll be able to watch the sunset over Mono Lake," Trisha said softly, looking out over the lake.

"Frazier, what kind of name is that, Scottish?" Trisha asked.

"You're right. You must know something about the derivation of names. Yep, the mighty Frazier clan from central and southern Scotland. We can date ourselves back to 1200 AD. And what about you? With whom am

I having this lovely dinner tonight?"

I was glad the opportunity to find out more about her presented itself.

"Keys, from the famous Keys family orange grovess of Southern California. We can date our oranges back to the late 1800's," she said with a big smile. "Actually, our ancestral family probably didn't live too far from yours. The name is English. In the times when life seemed much simpler, Miller's milled, Baker's baked and somewhere in there our family must have made keys...or so the story goes."

"Trisha Keys, originally from Southern California," I said as I put out my hand. "It's nice to meet you."

"Likewise, Vince Frazier, originally from Scotland," she said as her hand lightly gripped mine.

Her small warm hand was soft and inviting. We looked at each other for a moment while I held her hand as long as I dared.

"Then you're from Southern California?" I asked, as I slowly released her hand and wishing to find out more about this intriguing lady.

"Actually, I was raised and went to school in several towns, but all were in Orange Country, like our orange ranches once were."

"Once were?"

"Well, we do have some orange tree acreage left but most of our property was sold off over the years and replaced by shopping malls, homes, and oh yes, freeways."

"I'm sure the commuters driving to work at three miles an hour wished you'd sold all your land to Cal Trans for even more freeways. And where did you do your nursing?"

"I wanted to get away so I went even farther south to San Diego State University. At first, I found myself continuing my major in surfing. Eventually I settled down and finished both my B.A. and M.A. in Nursing," Trisha said proudly.

"And I thought that only the University of Hawaii awarded a B.A. in surfing."

"That was my second choice for schools. That really would have gotten me out of Orange County and there would be better surfing competitions too, but I probably wouldn't have graduated!"

"You competed?" I asked.

"Yep, I loved it and was pretty good, but I traded that life in for saving lives, or at least trying to."

Now I understood that lean but strong and athletic body, and the beach girl blond streaked hair which made her even more intriguing.

"What about you? Where did you live and go to school," Trisha asked with sincere interest.

"The City by the Bay...San Francisco. Looks like we both had our oceans, except yours was warmer. Then a B.A. in business at San Francisco State University and an M.B.A. not too far away at the University of San Francisco. So you can see why I'm a Giant and Forty-Niner fan," I added.

"Yeah, but I'd still prefer to watch a surfing competition at Sunset Beach!" Trisha said with a laugh.

"Well, are you about ready to order?" Paul asked, breaking the moment.

"Actually Paul, we may need a few more minutes to look at the menus…but please remind me of the specials for tonight."

"Our chef has two specials tonight. The first is a wonderful poached salmon served with wild rice and asparagus. The second is a flame broiled tri-tip sliced and served with a mushroom wine sauce, a baked potato, and a nice assortment of steamed vegetables," Paul proudly reported.

"The salmon sounds great to me!" Trisha announced.

"And the tri-tip with the mushroom wine sauce will hit the spot," I chimed in.

"How about that great Caesar Salad you mix and serve for two Paul? Does that sound okay with you, Trisha?"

"Perfect," she replied.

"This isn't what you expected for tonight, is it Trisha?" I asked cautiously.

"Actually, it's close to what I'd hoped for, but with a different person," she responded quietly.

"Well, I hope I'm at least an adequate substitute."

"More than adequate," she said softly.

The setting sun was starting to project orange onto the white clouds above the eastern shores of the lake.

The lake's blue waters also participated by reflecting both the white and orange sky across its immense surface.

"This is perfect," Trisha whispered. "Can we walk out on the porch for a moment before our meal arrives, to get a full view of the lake?"

"Sure, I'd like that. You really should get the full effect,"

We took the few steps out onto the porch almost in front of our window table. It was an explosive sunset

"I can't remember seeing a more brilliant sunset over Mono Lake than the one before us tonight," I stated.

"I've seen few anywhere that can even come close," Trisha returned.

We stood next to each other with our shoulders lightly touching. I felt my hand slowly clasp hers. I hadn't planned on it. It just seemed to happen, so I held on and gave a little squeeze.

Trisha looked ahead with a slight smile on her face, then lightly squeezed back.

With that, I smiled too.

Chapter Three

The Call

A loud ringing broke the silence. It seemed to be coming from the small black purse Trisha had carried out to the patio with her. She looked surprised and a little shaken as she pulled out her cell phone. Our hands pulled apart.

"Excuse me a moment, Vince," she said, as she walked a few feet away across the patio.

I stood for a moment looking out at the lake.

"Gary, where are you? . . .Then why didn't you at least call me earlier? . . .Yes, I'm still at Lee Vining. There is no way I could have driven back. ...Well, what kind of emergency...to help Julie... what?" Trish said, as she raised her voice.

At this point I realized Trisha needed her privacy so I made a quick exit back to our table.

From the window I could see her talking. I could tell she was irritated and upset, just as I would be in the same situation.

Paul walked by so I ordered a glass of the house

Cabernet. Since the bar was only twenty feet away, Paul brought it almost immediately.

I hoped Trisha was okay, and for a purely selfish reason I hoped this was enough of a problem to break up any romantic relationship she may have had with this guy Gary.

I sipped my wine as I realized how strong my reaction was to his call. I'd fallen for Trisha. I really like this Vegas emergency room nurse from the orange groves of Southern California. I've only known her for a few hours, yet I'm smitten! Even before I broke off my engagement with Shari a year ago, I'd never felt this way about her...even after two years of dating and that's exactly why I broke it off.

I could see Trisha slide the phone back into her purse. She looked irritated and a bit confused as she moved toward our table.

"Sorry about the call, Vince, but I needed a moment to deal with it," she said apologetically.

"I understand. Anything I can do to help?"

"You've already done so much...helping me keep my mind off my situation and bringing me to this charming place. I'd almost forgotten about..." she paused.

"Gary?" I asked.

"You heard?"

"Just the first few sentences before I came inside. Is he the no show if you don't mind my asking?"

"No, I really don't mind. I feel like I can share almost anything with you...but Gary...he's impossible!

23

He may soon to be my ex-boyfriend," she said, shaking her delicate head as her eyes started to water.

"Apparently, a friend named Julie had been thrown out of her apartment on Monday night and needed someone to help her with her things and a place to stay. It seemed that Gary quickly volunteered without bothering to let me know. He said he was so busy helping her that it slipped his mind to call. But it's okay, because he says he's sorry, . . .says he wants to see me. In the meantime, he has a house guest for a few days...and we both can guess who that is..." a frustrated Trisha stated.

"Well at least he is the kind of guy to help out a friend," I said, trying to make her feel better.

Then I realized that I was defending the creep, which I really didn't want to do.

"Yeah, but it turns out that Julie is an ex- girlfriend whom he's also been seeing the last five months since we started dating."

"Ouch, I'm sorry," was about all I could get out.

Paul arrived with our salad. He mixed the Caesar salad in a large bowl in front of us, carefully dividing it in half and placing it on two plates.

"Thanks Paul, that looks great," I said approvingly.

"Why are men like that? You know, rather thoughtless?" Trisha asked inquisitively.

I really didn't want to defend or explain all men, but I felt I at least should defend myself as a man.

"I hope most of us aren't that selfish and

thoughtless, Trisha."

"Have you ever done that to a woman, you know, forgotten to tell her some important details that could affect your relationship?"

I knew she was trying to work this thing through and was really asking these questions rhetorically as she tried to figure out what she was going to do.

"I sure hope I haven't...I'm basically a pretty honest and open person...Truth to me is very important...probably the most important ingredient in any meaningful relationship." I explained.

"You know, that's why I feel it's so easy for me to talk with you. Since I met you I've felt that I could trust you, that I could tell you, well, almost anything. That's one of the reasons I'm sitting here with you now," she said as she took a bite of her salad.

"And what is the other reason?" I found myself asking.

Trisha's laid her fork down and looked straight at me for a few moments. She reached over and gently placed her hand on mine.

"The other reason is because I really like you. When you first introduced yourself to me, even though I was upset, I got this feeling, like maybe everything was going to be all right. Maybe something special was about to happen...and has it?" she quietly asked.

I wasn't sure what to say. But I knew what she meant, and yeah, I'd felt that way too. Just after I saw the biker on Nicely's patio and the delicate features of

Trisha's face profiled by the blue sky, I knew I had to introduce myself, even if it was just to hear her voice.

"Since I saw you at Nicely's I haven't been able to think of much else," I said, throwing caution to the wind. "I sort of felt like we'd known each other for a long time, like we were old friends...and...much more than friends," I said gazing longingly into her eyes, our hands still pressed together.

"Now who gets the salmon? That's right, Trisha, and Vince you're the tri-tip," Paul unknowingly interrupted as he placed the plates in front of us.

"May I get you anything else?" he added.

"Would you like a glass of wine too?" I quietly asked Trisha.

"No thank you, Vince. I'm just fine the way things are," she responded.

We both began eating as if we were starving. I wasn't sure if it was because the food was so good, or our cheeseburgers at lunch really hadn't filled us up, or that we weren't quite sure what to say to each other after our candid expressions of mutual attraction.

From my standpoint, it was all three.

So, we sat there quietly eating, looking up periodically catching the other's gaze. Both of us knew it was good to just be sitting together. Both of us knew that something special was happening.

It was dark and cold as we walked out to my car. Trisha's shawl really came in handy. The stars were brilliant and looked like they were just a few feet away.

26

We both paused for a moment and looked at them. I quickly reached out in front of Trisha and pretended to grab one. I slowly brought back my closed hand.

"This is for you," I whispered, "a shining star, for a shining star."

She reached out tenderly to take my hand in hers.

"Does this mean I have a wish, a wish upon a star?" she asked.

"Of course," I responded.

With that she moved closer to me putting her arms over my shoulders as she gently touched her lips to mine.

"Then this is my wish," she said as she kissed me again.

It was both strange and fascinating. I felt her warmth against me as our bodies seemed to melt together.

"That would have been my wish too," I said as we slowly got into the car.

The drive back to the Murphy's Motel took only a few minutes. We both were silent. I was trying to figure out exactly where our relationship was going and what I should do next.

We found a place to park a room or two away from number 12. I turned off the engine. The interior had just warmed up from our short drive, so we both sat still.

"What are you going to do?" I finally asked, breaking the silence.

"About?" Trisha responded.

"About you and Gary and tomorrow," I queried

"I'm very confused. You've confused me, Vince...I'm not sure if my heart and head are working together right now. I do know my heart is working overtime," she said as she took my hand.

"I think I know what you mean. I'm feeling a lot of emotions right now too. It's happening so fast. I don't want to let this moment be a reaction to Gary's insensitivity towards you. I want it to stand on its own...you and me, because it's right for both of us," I said thoughtfully.

Trisha looked at me. I could tell she was confused. But her eyes also looked deep into mine in a warm and tender way, giving away her feelings for me.

"We probably should both get some sleep and talk in the morning," I reluctantly advised.

I really wanted more, much more of Trisha, yet I knew it wouldn't be right. Things needed to be worked out. Decisions needed to be made.

"I know you're right Vince. Things between us have happened fast and the thing with Gary..." Trisha paused.

"Let's get some sleep and work things out in the morning," I said as I went around and opened her car door.

We walked the few steps to her room. She took out her keys and unlocked the door. We both stood there for a moment. I reached out and tenderly pulled her towards me giving her a hug, then a kiss on her forehead as she looked up at me with those blue eyes.

"Vince, I need to tell you something about Gary and me...we...,"

"Trisha, Trisha, let's talk in the morning. How about 8:30 a.m. at Nicely's coffee shop?"

She nodded and gave me a big smile as she entered her room and closed the door.

Trisha understood. She knew how hard it was to say goodnight, and she knew it would only be harder if we stood there any longer.

My room, good old 23, was dark and cold. I quickly turned on the heater, took a warm shower, and got into bed. My mind was in shambles. I had a lot of things to sort out. I would be leaving tomorrow for Tuolumne Meadows Lodge for a couple more nights, and Trisha...Sleep! I must be alert tomorrow. I turned off the light and laid there in the dark. It was silent except for the occasional sound of an over anxious trucker speeding by. Then it became silent again.

Chapter Four

The Dilemma

I awoke at 7:00 a.m., washed up, and got dressed. I was both anxious and excited. Anxious because I didn't know what Trisha was going to do and excited because in a short time I'd be sitting across from her at Nicely's.

I walked to the mini mart at the Standard Station next door to the motel and picked up a *USA Today*. I continued to walk the two short blocks up to the restaurant. I took a booth next to the side window and ordered a cup of coffee. Then I picked up the paper and began to read the front page. Yet, if you'd asked me what I'd read, I couldn't tell you. My mind was wandering, thinking about all the possibilities regarding Trisha and me.

Although it was just 8:15, fifteen minutes before Trisha was to meet me, maybe she was as anxious to see me as I was to see her. Maybe she was on her way up the street right now.

I went out the front door and looked down the street. The highway was quiet except for a white sedan pulling out of the motel's parking lot and heading rapidly towards me. As I watched I could see that it was a Nissan Altima and Trisha was sitting in the driver's seat. She was moving way too fast to be able to turn into the restaurant.

Without thinking I jumped into the outside lane and began waving my arms. Trisha looked both startled and confused as she drove by. The car headed up the street another hundred feet when I saw the brake lights come on as the Altima started to slow and pull over to the side.

I was already running toward her when she stopped. The passenger side window rolled down as I leaned in breathing hard.

"Trisha, what are you doing? Where are you going?" I asked anxiously.

"Vince, I'm really confused. After I got back to my room Gary called again. He said that he wanted me to come right back to Vegas. I told him I thought I'd stay a while longer. He said if I didn't come home right away, he'd drive up and take me back. I really don't want to see Gary now, but I thought maybe I should go back and settle this right now," she said as tears filled her eyes.

"Trisha, please! Let's talk, let's talk," I pleaded softly and slowly trying to calm her down.

"Vince, you don't understand. I don't want you to be caught in the middle of this thing between Gary and me. I like you too much. Gary can be very hardheaded. He just might come here!"

"I'm not worried about Gary. I'm worried about you, Trisha. Please, just come inside. At least you have to eat some breakfast for the drive back," I said as convincingly as I could.

Trisha thought for a moment, then turned off the engine.

"You're right Vince. We should talk and I need a little coffee," she answered, getting out of the Altima and wiping her eyes with a tissue.

As we started the walk to Nicely's, I took her hand. She let me, so I continued to hold it until we arrived at the restaurant.

We got back to my table and I quickly asked the waitress for some water and a coffee for Trisha.

"Trisha, I don't want you to go back right now. I want you to stay. Gary's the one who didn't have the decency to let you know, after you drove eight hours from Vegas to meet him, that he wasn't going to be here. It seems to me that he's trying to control you. If you return to Vegas now, he'll always try to control you."

I tried to convince her with both concern and affection.

"I know you're right, but I didn't want you to get hurt, Vince."

"I understand Trisha, but I can take care of myself and I really think Gary was just trying to rile you so you'd do what he wanted."

"After what he did, and now demanding I come

back, I am angry enough to tell him what he can do with our relationship," Trisha added with a flip of her wrist.

"I really want you to stay. Besides, you planned to be here another two days, so why don't you? You could come up with me to Tuolumne Meadows Lodge. I have a tent cabin reserved there for two nights. It's a beautiful place and I'd love to show you around," I stated encouragingly.

"I've never been to that part of Yosemite and the last person I want to see now is Gary...You say you have a cabin for two nights?"

"Two," I said.

"Okay. Why not? I can't think of a better way to spend them than with you," she added.

"Funny thing Trisha, that's what I was just thinking too!"

I flashed a big smile which she immediately returned.

At the motel we packed up our things and put them in my Highlander. I went over to the office to see Betty.

"Good morning, Vince," Betty greeted when she saw me come through the door.

"Same to you. It has turned out to be a incredible day, Betty!"

"Heading on up the pass soon?" she replied.

"Yes, right away and I want to turn in the keys for my room as well as number twelve. Trisha Keys is checking out now too."

"Not to be prying, but I did see you two leave for

dinner last night. Looks like you have an attractive new friend," Betty commented.

"I'd have to say guilty as charged. She's quite a lady. By the way, do you mind if we leave her Altima here for a couple of days?" I asked.

"No, not at all. Just move it around back," she replied.

"Thanks a lot. I'll see you when I bring Trisha back."

"I need to stop at the Mobil station."

Trisha moved her car to the back of the Murphy's Motel and we headed south on Highway 395 to the 120 junction about a mile up the road.

"I need to stop for a moment at the Mobil station and fill up, Trisha. While I'm doing that you just might like to check this place out," I added with a smile.

As we pulled in Trisha saw what I meant.

"Is that he station also a restaurant and shop?" she

34

asked surprised

"Well actually a market, deli, gift shop, and sporting goods store,...and they sell gas," I enthusiastically replied.

"This may take a moment," Trisha yelled back, as she quickly headed in the door.

Now I could see how she managed to get through the massive factory discount stores in Barstow on her way up to Lee Vining in just an hour. She moves fast!.

I filled up, cleaned off the windows, and started towards the station when Trisha stepped out.

"That's an amazing place and the sandwiches looked gigantic! Too bad it's not time for lunch," Trisha said with delight.

"Wait till our next stop, Trisha," I said mysteriously.

Trisha looked over at me with a rather expectant look on her face that turned into a big eager smile.

As we drove up Lee Vining Canyon to Tioga Pass, Trisha took my hand.

It was an incredible day mainly because I had Trisha with me! The sky was a deep blue and the canyon was stunning. I never would have thought that my hiking buddy would change from my brother to this amazing woman in just a couple of days. There was so much I wanted to show her, so much I wanted to ask, so much I wanted to share.

We passed Ellery Lake near the summit and stopped in a little valley that held the Tioga Pass Resort. There was a little store, café, and a dozen cabins scattered along a small creek, quaint and picturesque.

"Now why don't we grab an early lunch here? The food is great! They even do their own baking, if you like pie and things like that," I added.

"I've been known to bite into a good piece of pie every now and then, even without much encouragement. This place is wonderful!"

We sat at the counter in the small café and ordered the split pea soup and salad combo. It didn't take a bit of encouragement for Trisha to order a piece of peach pie and I had mine a la mode.

We sat quietly eating our soup and salads. It wasn't hard to tell that Trisha was really enjoying her meal.

"You sure know all the right spots that make a girl feel very special," Trisha said as she spun around once on her counter stool.

"Vince, I'm glad we're doing this, doing this together. I'm really excited. I feel like a school girl on a first date. Yet, with you I feel so comfortable I can totally be myself and not worry."

"I'm glad Trisha. I can't believe we're here together. I can't wait to share all this with you and find out more about you," I replied.

"About that sharing, do you want some of my ice cream on your pie?" I asked, holding up a spoonful.

"Don't mind if I do," she returned and I plopped some on the side of her plate as she spun around again.

Tioga Pass into Yosemite National Park at 9,945 feet is the highest highway pass in the Sierras. We stopped for a moment at the entrance as I displayed my National Park Pass and then drove in a few hundred feet to a scenic pull out and parking area.

Past the meadow was a stand of fir trees against the base of snow-covered Mount Dana which rose to 13,000 feet above us.

"I sure wish I had a camera," Trisha said as though talking to herself.

"Coming right up," I said as I grabbed my iPhone which seldom left my side when I hiked and fished.

I backed up a couple of feet and took a great picture of Trisha with Mount Dana in the background.

"Now I want to get one of you," she stated as she took the phone from me and snapped the shot.

"Aah, a moment in time for posterity," she said as she looked at the picture on the LED screen. "You know, you're not bad looking with wavy brown hair, deep blue eyes, nice build at about six feet plus. That's enough to make any girl on your arm feel special."

She handed me the camera and looped her arm through mine.

"Now I feel special," I replied, as I turned her around and preceded to give her a long kiss.

Her lips eagerly returned my affection. For a moment we just stood together.

"Wow," she said. "I sure hope there's more where that came from."

"There is. I've been saving up just for you," I returned with a slight laugh and smile.

Chapter Five

The Lodge

We drove the nine miles off the pass along Dana Fork, watching the creek meander and gradually fall beside us, before we arrived at the short turnoff to Tuolumne Meadows Lodge. We parked in the large parking lot from which we could see the white canvas tent cabins scattered up the meadow and into the granite and trees. Along the parking lot were large green metal boxes.

"What are the green boxes for?" Trisha asked curiously.

"Those are where the lodge guests keep their food and fragrant cosmetic supplies to discourage the local black bears from visiting their cabins and cars at night. They're made of thick metal and have a latch system that they say is bear proof. We'll keep the snacks I brought in there along with anything that has a fragrance that may attract them.

I could see Trisha squirm a bit.

"To keep the bears out? Do they actually come into

your cabin?" she asked concerned.

"I haven't seen one up here my last few visits, but they have gone into one or two cabins at night in the past when the occupants have kept food. They prefer to break into cars when they smell something, but that probably happens just a few times each summer."

Trisha sat quietly for a moment, obviously thinking about the possibilities of an unwelcome meeting with a bear.

We walked to the Lodge, which was basically a combination wood and canvas structure that housed a kitchen, dining room and reception area.

We walked to the Lodge.

This is rustic, but beautiful. It reminds me of a summer camp I once stayed at as a child. We slept in wood buildings," she stated.

"Then you've roughed it before?" I asked. "When I was very young our family did go camping a couple of times near Big Bear Lake, but we stayed in a large camper truck. I did really enjoy it!" she exclaimed.

I think she was trying to make me feel better about the "rustic" part.

We entered the small reception area and approached the counter. Right away I saw a couple of familiar faces.

"Hey Danny, it's good to see you," I said enthusiastically.

Danny, a redhead in his thirties with a big smile, responded, "Mr. Frazier, it's great to see you!"

"Vince," I said, using the old punch line, "Mr. Frazier is my dad. How have you been since I saw you at the Ahwahnee in the valley back in April? Is everything going all right?"

"It sure is! I'm glad you were able to make it up again this summer."

Then I noticed Rhea at the computer behind him look around.

"Good to see you too, Rhea."

She smiled and waved over her shoulder.

"I brought a new friend with me this summer. I'd like you to meet Trisha," I continued as Trisha reached out her hand.

"Very nice to meet you Trisha," Danny said shaking her hand.

"She's obviously not your brother and she's much

cuter," he added with a laugh, as a slightly embarrassed Trisha smiled back.

"Trisha has volunteered to be his replacement since he couldn't make it. This is her first time here and I can't wait to show her around."

"Do the bears ever really bother anyone here?" Trisha asked, apparently still quite concerned about them.

"So far we've only seen a couple wander through the area one night about a week ago, but they were just passing through checking things out. I assure you, if they were a big problem, you wouldn't find me at the Lodge! I'd still be down in the valley at the Ahwahnee Hotel," Danny added, trying to alleviate some of Trisha's concerns.

"Well thanks, Danny. I'm just not used to spending the night with bears," Trisha returned.

"You know, Trisha, with their nice fur coats, they can take the chill off at night if you snuggle up to them really close," I stated with a big smile, at which point I got a good punch in the arm.

"I had hoped to get extra body heat from somewhere else," she quietly whispered in my ear.

"Cabin ready?" I asked.

"Sure is. You've got 10, first one up the hill, on the granite, next to the river," Danny said as he pointed out the window.

"That's one of my favorites! I'm glad it's available. Thanks Danny."

"If I can do anything for you just let me know," he returned as we headed out the door and up the hill.

The water of the Dana Fork was splashing between the rocks as it flowed down beside us. A little-ways up the footpath near our cabin, we could see and hear its waterfall.

The water of the Dana Fork was splashing between the rocks.

"Music to put you to sleep at night," I said as I opened the unlocked wooden screen door to Number 10.

Trisha slowly walked inside. It was obvious that she was a bit confused. The cabin was quite light because the sun shone through its canvas sides.

"Where is the light switch?"

"Oh, there is no electricity in the tent cabins, only in

the Lodge and the restrooms down the hill," I explained.

"Restrooms down the hill?" she asked.

Then she looked around the cabin taking in the two single and one double cots, card table, and chair that furnished our room.

Then she looked around the cabin.

"Down the hill?" she repeated.

"It's only a couple hundred feet away, common facilities. They do have a men's side and a women's side with flush toilets," I added, but I don't think it made Trisha feel much better.

"We light the cabin with those candles on the table. And we heat it with that neat dark tin wood burning stove. You might say it's rustic, but it can be very romantic," I added, trying to lighten the obvious shock.

"You mean late at night, when I need to go, I have to walk a couple hundred feet through the dark and possibly by bears to use the restroom?" she asked turning to look at me.

"Oh no, Trisha, not in the dark. I brought a couple of flashlights along. You want yours now?"

I felt that this was probably a good time for a hug as I reached out and put my arms around her, her mouth still hanging open in disbelief.

We stood there for a moment as her eyes moved down to the cement floor only partially covered by an old woven rug. After a moment she broke the silence.

"Then how do we keep the bears out?"

"Well, you really don't if they want to come in, but you can hook the screen door shut from the inside at night if you want."

Bears and security were still a major concern I noted.

"You used the term rustic a while ago. I think a better way to describe it is ancient, Vince. And why do they call this place a lodge?"

"That's a good question Trisha. I never could figure that one out either. I think they use the term very loosely," I noted with a big smile.

Trisha slumped down on one of the cots.

"Oh, you're picking that one?" I stated, as I received another punch, this time in the leg.

"Trisha, this place is incredible! It grows on you. You'll see. Let's bring things in from the car and drive down to the meadows. I want to show you something."

"Okay," she returned unenthusiastically. "I can't wait for it to grow on me...I hope it happens soon!".

We drove the mile down the hill to Tuolumne Meadows. To our right a giant granite dome appeared. To our left we could see the Tuolumne River. In front of us a large and beautiful meadow appeared.

"That massive granite dome is called Lembert Dome. If we get a chance we can climb to its top. A great view! And over there are the headwaters of the Tuolumne River, where it officially starts its hundred plus mile journey down the mountains, through Modesto, and out into the bay," I stated in my best travel guide voice.

"It's really amazing, almost overwhelming! And what's that?" Trisha enthusiastically asked as we drove across the Tuolumne River bridge.

"Well that's the general store and café. Would you like to stop and take a look?"

"Of course, Vince. You're getting to know me pretty well," she replied, as we pulled over and parked.

It didn't take Trisha long to check out the place. It was a rather "rustic" market-sporting goods store for the local campers which included a small café ice cream shop for when they got tired of cooking over an open fire or camp gas stove.

"Trisha, I really want you to take a short hike with me out through the meadows," I stated.

"Sounds wonderful to me," Trish responded.

Chapter Six

Closer to You

We drove another mile passing the visitor's center and parked along the meadow where another granite dome shot up.

"Trisha, this is Pothole dome on the west side of the meadows. A gentle trail goes to the river and canyon from here. I want to share this with you."

I took her hand in mine as we walked through the dark green meadow grass and wildflowers.

Several mountain peaks shot up around us, but the distant Cathedral Peak with its sharp rocky surface covered with snow stood out.

"This is breathtaking, like out of a fairytale," Trisha said as her light blue eyes sparkled in the sunlight.

We left the path and walked along the meadow as it moved into a forest of firs.

"Stop!" I whispered softly but firmly. "Look down by your feet to the left."

Trisha's eyes grew big and lit up even more.

"He's amazing," she said quietly as she intently watched the little spotted fawn try to hide himself in the high meadow grass.

"He's so still! All you can see are his short quick breathing movements," Trisha continued.

"Yes, he's perfect and doing exactly what nature intended when she gave him that spotted brown and white camouflage so he would not be seen when he lays still. His mother left him to hide in this dark green grass, not expecting anyone would venture off the path. I'm sure she's watching us from the forest right now, very concerned. And he's probably as scared as can be. We'd better move away slowly."

We took one last look and walked towards the path leading to a spot where the meadow met the river.

"That was incredible!" Trisha said as she squeezed my hand.

"One of the many benefits of Yosemite," I returned.

The Tuolumne River dropped from the meadow down a sloping canyon as it leaped from one beautiful waterfall and granite pool to the next. The water in the granite pools had a clear emerald glow, unusual for high mountain rivers.

We sat on an old fallen tree overlooking one of the falls.

"This is a fairy tale, and I feel like the princess with her prince. It's all so peaceful and relaxing, like it's been here for thousands of years and will be here for at least a thousand more. It's a place I'd come if I want to forget about everything else," Trisha said almost reverently.

"It's been a special place for millions of years, especially now since I'm here sharing this with you, my Princess Trisha," I said as we both turned to each other at the same time and kissed.

"I wish we were back at our cabin, even that tent cabin," she whispered as she gently bit my ear.

I kissed her again and said with a smile, "We'll be back at the 'lodge' very soon."

We both started to laugh.

It was late afternoon by the time we got back to the "lodge."

"Trisha, do you want to take a shower before we go to dinner at 6:30? It will still be light?"

"And what waterfall do I stand under?" she asked.

"I guess I deserve that," I laughed. "The showers in the bathroom aren't bad. Here's a furnished towel, a bar of soap, and you may want to change while you're there. Be sure to put on a warm coat and practical shoes for the walk back. The ground is rocky and uneven and it's going to be chilly tonight."

"Yes sir," Trisha returned, with a salute.

I shaved and showered and dressed warmly, putting on my blue shirt and sweater. and headed back to the room. Then I filled the furnished stainless steel water pitcher from a nearby outlet and opened a bottle of Merlot. I took the plastic wrappers off our "glasses" and opened a box of Wheat Thins after lighting candles.

"Oh, you left the light on," Trisha said smiling as she

opened the screen door. "That's another experience I'll have to put in my diary of memorable events. The woman in the shower next to me kept turning her water off and on, so mine kept going from hot to cold. When she started to sing, I knew it was time to leave! Oh, wine and crackers...and candle light, what more could a girl ask for."

Trisha paused and batted her eyes.

"Nothing more than you deserve," I returned.

"You mean I deserve all this?" she said as she looked around.

"And much more," I added.

"I'm glad you said that Vince. Now I can't wait to hear about dinner. Do we bring the crackers?"

"Nah, just your appetite, a friendly smile, and your gift for gregarious conversation."

"What does that mean, Vince?"

"Well, we don't entirely eat alone. They seat us at table for nine, and although we order our own entrée, we share the bread basket, salad, and soup bowl. It's kind of a modified Basque style restaurant."

Trisha thought about this for a moment and adjusted her anticipated vision of a candle light dinner for two at a secluded table. That would have been my choice for tonight too.

"Then chocolate mousse for dessert is definitely out?" she asked with a twinkle in her eye.

"That would be my bet," I returned.

"I guess it's good I took a partially cold shower then.

It will keep we awake for the conversation...actually, come to think of it, it could be fun."

"Another memory for your diary?" I asked.

"Hopefully not an entry for the 'Things I really Want To Forget' section," she returned.

The dinner was very nice. We sat with a group of three hikers out of Los Angeles who were doing the High Sierra Camp loop for a week and two other couples. One elderly couple from Fresno was visiting the lodge for their forty second time and reliving past memories. The other couple, from Palm Desert, was in their thirties excited about being at the lodge and anxious to hit the trail up to Vogelsang Lake in the morning.

Trisha seemed to enjoy the meal and the conversation. She especially enjoyed talking with the Jarrens from Palm Desert. Jack turned out to be a plastic surgeon and Sharon, his wife, was an emergency room nurse! Needless to say, the shop talk went on forever, but I contributed too, when I found out that Jack was an avid fly fisherman.

"Vince, that was nicer than I had expected. Even though I wanted to spend that time with you, it was kind of fun to meet new people."

"I look forward to the meals just for that reason. You meet people from all around the world. Years ago, I even met a young Middle Eastern journalist who was on leave from covering the war in Iraq for CNN. She was meeting a friend here, just to clear her mind," I replied.

It was around 8:30 p.m. The darkness and cold had quickly come in.

"Man, it's cold," Trisha said. zipping up her jacket all the way to her chin and slowly turning in a circle as she saw the night sky.

"Look at those stars! I bet we can see almost all of them!"

"Do you want another wish?" I asked. "We're even closer to the stars now."

"Yeah, if we could only wear stars like diamonds."

"That's an unusual saying. I like it," I returned.

"My grandmother used to say that when we walked the orange groves at night in southern California. It's for wishes. She felt that if we could wear stars, then we would not only look beautiful, but we could pull a star off our necklace anytime we needed and make a wish, as many as we wanted."

"That's wonderful, Trisha. Your grandmother must have been quite a lady."

"She was Vince. She really was."

Chapter Seven

Fire and Candles

"Come on Trisha, I want you to see the campfire," I said as she followed me through the dark.

"One night I sat over there by the fire next to a man who turned out to be an Astro Physicist. Apparently, he was considered to be one of the world's most knowledgeable scientists on black holes in space. He also knew the location of all the satellites. We counted the shining movement of twelve that night as they orbited above us. Matter of fact Trisha, look over there," I said as I pointed at what looked like a fast moving star crossing the sky.

"That's incredible. I didn't know you could actually see them," she said with her head tilted way back.

"Hey city girl, all those Vegas lights block out the real light show."

"I see what you mean," she said as she searched the sky for other satellites.

We sat on one of the benches that had been placed in a circle around the outdoor campfire for the lodge guests to enjoy. Its flames were bright and warm. Trisha cuddled up close to me.

There was a couple helping their two children roast marshmallows over the fire using bent wire coat hangers. Once the marshmallow was a warm golden brown, they'd sandwich it between two Graham crackers alongside a piece of milk chocolate candy bar and gobble the sticky treat up.

"Would you like to try to make a s'more mister? We have a lot of marshmallows and chocolate," the young boy asked.

"Trisha, you want to try?"

"Sure! Thank you, young man. It looks delicious," she said as he handed her the hanger and a marshmallow.

"And what's your name?" Trisha asked the young boy.

"Eddie," he replied.

"Well, I'm Trisha and this is Vince," she returned with a gentle smile.

"It's not as easy as it looks Trisha," I said as she quickly pushed the marshmallow through the tip of the wire and stuck it into the flames.

As it became a small ball of fire, I continued, "They have a tendency to burn unless you hold it a bit away from the glowing embers and stay away from the fire."

Trisha pulled the flaming ball of marshmallow out of the fire and attempted to blow it out. On her third hard puff the fire went out, leaving a blackened marshmallow barely hanging onto the tip of her wire. Suddenly, it plopped to the ground in front of her.

I could see the disappointed look on her face as she looked down at the dirt and marshmallow mixture at her feet.

"Darn," she said.

"Trisha, you have to be very careful with the marshmallows and hold them near the embers so they won't catch fire and burn. It took me a while to figure it out too," Eddie said, trying to cheer her up. I don't think the expert advice of a eight year old made her feel any better.

"Okay Trisha, try again," I said as Eddie passed her another marshmallow.

"I'll take my time and look for the embers this time," she said with determination.

She turned the marshmallow around slowly above the embers and within a minute her marshmallow was a golden brown.

"Looks like you're ready for the chocolate and Graham crackers" Eddie said, which she took and sandwiched around her golden marshmallow.

Trisha looked at it for a moment and took a bite.

"Hey, that's pretty darn good! Thanks Eddie," she said as she pressed it up to my mouth.

I took a bite and smiled

"Perfect! Not too dark, not to light, a perfect s'more," I said as Trisha smiled, ate the rest, and licked her fingers.

We sat there for a few moments watching the smoke spiral into the starry sky.

"And what are your favorite things to do?" Trisha asked as she leaned even harder against me, "besides watch me make s'mores?"

"Well, this is on the top of my list, but I really do like the Forty -Niners," I answered and received an elbow in my side.

"But honestly, I love to hike these mountains, see and feel their quiet but intense beauty all around me. I've also been known to swing a golf club and on the same day play a good game of tennis. And I've even been known to turn a TV on to a surfing competition now and again. Come to think of it, now I know where I've seen you before," I said as I pulled my arms in close to my sides for protection, only to feel a slight kick against my leg.

"And what about you, what do you like to do, besides hit that is?"

"If you had an older brother who for his tenth birthday wanted a razor cut and a tattoo, you'd learn to hit too! Actually, I've always liked water sports, swimming, water polo, surfing. I also love to dance and I do some biking."

"You're a real lady jock. I bet you'll hike the legs off me tomorrow." I said

"We're going hiking tomorrow?"

"That's what we came here for. Besides if you liked what you saw today, a stroll tomorrow along the Lyell

Fork should be a real treat!"

"I think I'm ready for just about anything with you Vince. Besides that will give us a good chance to talk some more, and I think the time is right for me to share some things about me I've not shared yet with you," Trisha softly whispered in my ear.

"And I want to share more with you too. Are you about ready to turn in?" I asked.

"Yeah, it's really chilly out here, although I'd like to go by way of the restroom. I don't want to have to take any midnight runs through bear country to use the facilities tonight," she added as I handed her the largest flashlight.

"Fine, then grab what you need from the cabin and I'll meet you there in a few minutes," I returned as I tossed another log onto the fire.

"Thanks a lot for the lesson, Eddie. The s'more was really good," she yelled back, as her flashlight disappeared into the night.

What a lady I thought. I have fallen for her. Why didn't I meet her ten years ago? There is so much I want to tell her, so much I want to share with her, but I know we both have some things we have to work out.

I headed up to the tent cabin. Trisha had already left for the lady's room. So I lit several candles and started a fire in our stove to take the deep chill off. I stripped down to my boxers and a T shirt and climbed in the double cot trying to keep warm.

Within a couple of minutes Trisha was back,

rubbing her hands together as she headed towards the stove.

"No bears, but it's freezing out there. And I could have sworn that same lady's back in the shower singing again!"

"Take your pick of the cots, there's two left," I said as Trisha began pulling off her clothes. The candle light bounced off her body, alternating light with shadow as she moved. It was captivating. Her body was tan, yet full in all the right places, athletic, yet delicate and sensuous. I couldn't take my eyes off her. She quickly dropped a pink nightgown over her head.

"Then I choose yours," she said as she jumped into my cot.

"Are you sure you should be here with me?" I asked softly.

"There's no place else I'd rather be," she said as she wrapped herself around me.

"Besides, it's freezing out there and every survival guide I've ever read says that the best way to survive is by sharing body heat. So hold me and give some up," Trisha continued as she slowly kissed my forehead.

"So you read several survival guides?" I softly whispered as we came nose to nose.

"Yes, but only the part about the body heat. I wanted to make sure I got it right," she whispered back as she looked into my eyes.

"I believe you have, and I think it's working," I whispered, "but no matter how badly I want you right now, I think we should wait. I don't want confusion and emotions to overshadow reason."

"You're right, Vince. Things are moving fast. So hold me... hold me close," she whispered back as I felt her warm lips pressed against mine.

I felt dizzy and amazed. It all seemed surreal. At the same time it seemed like we were meant to have been together since birth.

Even though I could hear a light wind outside and the falls just beyond our cabin, just before we fell asleep in each others arms, I believe I heard Trisha say with her last waking breath, "I love you Vince. I love you."

I awoke with Trisha still in my arms. I could feel the freezing air from our 9000 feet elevation. The summer warmth would come, but not until the sun was much higher in the sky.

I carefully rolled Trisha away, pulled on my jeans, some socks, and a warm coat, and then went to work on the stove that had gone out long ago. I knew Trisha would appreciate having a warm cabin and the ice cap on our pitcher of water melted away.

"Vince," Trisha said, "it was wonderful."

I stopped and leaned down caressing her head with my hands I kissed her cheek and said, "Men would fight wars for a night with you, dear Trisha."

Chapter Eight

Choices

Fighting the cold, I headed down to the men's room to shave and freshen up a bit. Only one or two other people appeared to be up.

It was a cloudless morning. Only the smoke from the cabins that were also seeking heat floated out above the trees. It was another morning in paradise, another moment I wanted to share with Trisha.

As I headed back to the cabin, I passed a man who looked a bit confused. His eyes locked on mine.

"Do you know which cabin is cabin 10?" he asked rather abruptly,

"Just up the hill," I responded. "Why do you want to know?"

"That's my business, not yours," he returned.

"Ten's my cabin so it is my business," I replied firmly.

"Is your name Frazier? Vince Frazier?" he asked.

Before I could answer he continued, "Since the motel room was in my name the lady who managed it told me that Trisha was probably up here with you."

"Then you're Gary?"

"Yeah, so step aside. I'm here to take her back."

"She's told me several times that she doesn't want to see you right now," I returned, holding my ground.

"Look, I drove all night to take her back to Vegas with me and that's what I'm going to do," Gary said as he pushed me aside.

When his arm hit me, I took hold of it and spun him around.

"Hang on! I don't want a problem here. I'll go talk to Trisha and see if she wants to see you," I said calmly as I saw his face redden.

With that, he quickly brought up his right fist. I turned and blocked his punch.

Just at that moment stepping from the cabin, Trisha yelled. "Gary! No! Don't!"

But it was too late. His left fist headed towards my right cheek. Again, I spun and blocked the punch.

"Gary," I shouted. "Just back off and we'll talk!"

This time he charged with both fists swinging.

I ducked, but took a glancing blow to the back of my head. I'd had enough.

I spun around and sent a snapping turn kick into his chest knocking him backwards onto the ground.

"Vince, don't hurt him," I heard Trisha yell as she came closer.

Gary lay on the ground trying to catch his breath.

"Gary, don't get back up. You can't win! My Special

Forces training will see to that. It's over!"

"Not until I get my fiancé," Gary said, trying to catch his breath.

"Your what?" I said in disbelief.

By now Trisha was kneeling down near Gary checking to see if he was all right.

As I looked down at her, she looked up at me with tears in her eyes.

"Vince, that's one of the things I wanted to tell you, one of the things I needed the right time to tell you," she cried.

"Then Gary is your..."

"Yes, but it's not all as it seems," she softly returned.

"Then what's all this about Gary being a no show so he could be with his ex- girlfriend?" I asked as I looked at Gary and tried to make sense out of it.

"Julie? Yeah, she is my ex-girlfriend from several years ago. Now she's Trisha's best friend and the Maid of Honor at our wedding next month. She had just lost her apartment and had to leave town on a business trip in a couple of days. She had a lot of our wedding stuff in it so I helped her move it into mine until Trisha came back," Gary said firmly as he got up and brushed the dirt off.

"Trisha, is this all true?" I asked, as my eyes locked on hers with obvious disappointment.

"Yes, but there is more to all this. I need to explain things to you," she cried softly.

"Then you lied to me Trisha! It all was a lie," I said.

"No Vince, I never lied to you. I...I just didn't tell you everything and how things really stood with Gary," Trisha struggled to say.

"What do you mean, how things really stood with me?" Gary chimed in.

"We need to talk too, Gary. I need to tell you how I really feel," Trisha said more firmly.

"Trisha, these few days were supposed to be our engagement get away celebration, and now...I had to help Julie! You'd want me to," he pleaded.

"No, you're right Gary. I'm glad you helped her but I was still upset with the situation... until..." Trisha paused.

"Until what?" Gary asked.

"Until I met Vince," Trisha answered as she looked into my eyes.

"I've had some doubts about us for some time now," Trish continued, "but things were happening so fast, I was confused. I had hoped to tell you about it when we were together in Lee Vining."

"Trisha...I've got to think...I can't believe this is happening," Gary muttered. "Is there somewhere I can clean up a bit?"

"Yeah, the restroom's just down the path and to the right," I offered as I pointed and Gary slowly moved away.

I was confused too and even felt a little sorry for Gary. I knew I loved Trisha; however, she'd lied to me or at least misled me...badly! Trust is so important to me. I felt betrayed and angry! Yet, my heart yearned for her and the time we'd spent together. It was a toxic mixture of emotions.

"I wanted to tell you, I tried to tell you, but you and I happened so fast! Gary pushed the engagement on me way too soon. I didn't know what to do! I was confused. I guess I was a coward and didn't want to hurt Gary and tell him that I must not love him enough to get married. That's what I was going to do when you stopped my car."

"Trisha, I don't know what to believe. I feel you misled me and weren't honest with me. You said you felt you could tell me anything, yet..."

"Vince, I can and I do feel that way. I tried...but it just didn't want to come out...I didn't want to possibly change how we were feeling...how I was feeling about you."

"How do I know what you told me was true?" I asked, trying to understand how Trisha really felt.

"Everything I told you about my life, about how I felt about you, about us, was true. Even last night when I whispered that I loved you...I really do Vince," she said gently.

She had said it. It wasn't the wind or the river.

It was Trisha saying it... and now she just said she loved me again!

"Trisha, I want to believe you. I want to be with you, but...engaged to be married? I don't know what to say, what to do right now. Speaking of things happening too fast!"

"Oh Vince, I want us to be together. I'll go with Gary, talk to him, and tell him that I don't want to marry him. Then we can talk things through when we're not confused and moving so fast. Vince, please," Trisha said, almost begging.

"What are you going to do, Trisha? Are you going to drive back with me?" Gary asked, returning after having had a few moments to think things through.

"Yes, Gary, we need to talk and I need to straighten everything out at home. I'll go and get my suitcase from the cabin. I also need to call Murphey's Motel and ask them to return my rental car."

"Sorry about the fight, Vince. I was so angry and so frustrated when Trisha didn't come back to Vegas. Then when I heard she was up here with you...I...."

"Apology accepted. I think I know how you feel. I can tell you really care about her, and I can see why. She's a beautiful lady...and well, sorry I took you down so hard."

"Yeah! Were you really Special Forces or was that just to keep me down?" he asked.

"Yep, that was my first graduate degree so to speak after college," I replied.

"Then I'm glad I stayed down...I wasn't feeling like I wanted to get up anyway after I hit that granite and dirt," he said with a slight smile.

I kind of liked the guy and knew he was going to have to do some fast talking all the way back to Vegas.

What was going to happen, I wasn't sure.

"I'm ready Gary. I just need a minute with Vince," Trisha said as she approached.

"I'll see you in the parking lot. I'm parked next to the first big green box," Gary said as he slowly moved down the hill.

"Vince, I need to do this. I want you to know that I really don't want to go. My heart is here with you, and taking that hike along Lyell Fork. Please Vince Frazier from Scotland, come to me," she said as she placed a piece of paper with her address and phone number in my hand.

With that Trisha came close, kissed my cheek, and whispered into my ear, "Men would fight wars for a night with you, dear Trisha...fight for me Vince, please fight for me," she said as she moved away.

Chapter Nine

Love or Forget

A feeling of emptiness hit me. My plans of discovery and sharing with Trisha were pulled out from under me. I felt like I'd walked down a busy street and into a silent and dark alley, alone.

I wasn't sure what I thought. Speaking of confusion and happening too fast.... I knew I needed time to sort things out, time to think. I still had several days I could be gone from work, and another night at the Lodge. I couldn't think of a better place to work things through than here in Tuolumne Meadows.

Breakfast, I thought, as reason began to take over. I need to eat before they close the kitchen until dinner. I headed toward the restaurant thinking that at least I had a beautiful day and my fly pole to keep me company. With that I began to chuckle as I envisioned how my fly pole could possibly take the place of Trisha.

"Good morning Vince," Danny said as I passed the registration counter.

"Same to you Danny, but I'll probably feel a bit

better after I get some breakfast in me," I replied.

I know he noticed that Trisha wasn't with me and, being the gentleman he was, had decided not to say anything.

As I put my name on the waiting list, I saw Jack and Sharon Jarren come in behind me and put their names on the list too. I knew this would be awkward.

"So you're all ready for your hike up to Vogelsang Lake today?" I asked with a smile.

"We sure are," Sharon responded with a big smile and a slight wiggle.

"It's going to be a long day hike, about fourteen miles if we don't get side tracked. The scenery and views are well worth it," Jack added as he looked around probably trying to spot Trisha.

"Well my plans changed," I stated, trying to fend off the obvious question.

"Trisha had to leave and go back to Vegas early this morning," I continued, "so I'll probably do a little fishing on the Lyell Fork or maybe run up to the pass and fish the Gaylor Basin."

"Oh, is everything all right with Trisha?" a disappointed Sharon quickly asked.

"She's fine. She just had some personal business to take care of," I returned with as much of a smile as I could muster.

"Sorry to hear that. We really enjoyed meeting her last night. She's quite a lady," Jack said while looking towards Sharon as their eyes met for a brief second.

"Hey Vince, why don't you join us to Vogelsang? I know with your hiking skills you won't slow us down," Jack stated with a smile.

Sharon too was smiling in obvious agreement.

"You could show me that back hand flip toss we talked about last night since I'm taking my fly pole too," he continued enthusiastically.

"I'd love to, but I have some serious thinking to do today. I need some quiet therapy time with my fly pole to work some things out, but I really appreciate the invitation. I'll probably see you here tonight for a late dinner. I'll want to hear how the hike went," I replied.

That evening we ended up seated at different tables. I made the usual conversation without really listening or knowing what I said. My mind was elsewhere. I ate quickly, smiled a lot, and went back to the cabin.

In the morning, the cabin seemed like a hollow shell. The excitement and joy of its "rustic" amenities had melted away. Trisha wasn't there to share them.

I grabbed my day pack, fishing gear, and pole, and headed down the trail across Dana Fork and on to Lyell. I looked down at the crystal-clear water that splashed across the large granite boulders under the walking bridge. The water reflected its light emerald color, but it wasn't quite as bright as yesterday's.

I followed Lyell upstream about half a mile, occasionally tossing in my fly at a few reliable spots, but to no avail. The trout weren't interested, nor was I.

How did this happen? Why were Trisha and I apart?

Did she really mislead me or was I so blinded by her I just wasn't listening well enough. Could I ever trust her again? Should I even bother to see her again? Thoughts raced through my head faster than I could gather and process them.

I knew we were attracted to each other from our first encounter at Nicely's Barbecue. Over dinner we began to feel that we were meant to be together. The star I grabbed and her wish and kiss were signs that brought us even closer together.

I remembered that she tried to tell me something at her motel room door, but I cut her off, afraid that it might bring us too close too soon and I would not want to say goodnight.

Then there was her confusion but also her determination to do the right thing for Gary and leave for Vegas the next morning to work things out with him.

And I knew she only stopped when she saw me because she cared about me and didn't want me to be caught in the middle of her breakup.

Then there was the magical day and night we spent together. Everything was exciting. Everywhere we looked we saw beauty, our eyes as wide open as our hearts.

The dinner, the stars, s'mores, and campfire all tied the knot between us even tighter. Her delicate grace and beauty reflected in the cabin's candlelight that almost overpowered my very being...and the night with Trisha in my arms...while in the morning, realizing it wasn't a dream when I awoke, and she was still there...in my arms...

I knew it wasn't working. Even the meandering river and my fly pole couldn't take my mind off Trisha. I needed to find a place that would completely have me focused on something else...I needed to get back to work.

I pulled out of the Lodge parking lot about noon, after saying a quick good by to Danny and Rhea. The drive down Tioga Pass Road to the entrance seemed to take forever. The high country's beauty was betrayed as my mind continued to be focused on Trisha.

Was Trisha just an encounter, or was something meant to come from all this?

I picked up my cell phone.

"Hey Larry. It's me, Vince. How is everything going?" I asked.

"You're glad I called, why?....You mean the Gallo reward trip for twenty employees we booked to Fiji for seven days?..... Jason is sick and can't go to take care of things for them? ....Then who's going? Somebody has to go. Gallo's too big a client to....Wait Larry, I'm coming back early, so I'll go. They leave on Thursday... tomorrow!.....Okay, I'll pick the paper work up from the office this afternoon and meet them all at the San Francisco Airport by 6:00 a.m."

Ouch! This would be close, but it sure snapped me out of my quandary.

It was dark as I drove toward San Francisco from

Modesto at 4:00 a.m. the next morning. Focused on the trip I hadn't had much time to think about Trisha, but now she kept floating in and out of my thoughts.

The commuter traffic from the Central Valley into the Bay Area was already starting to build up. The twelve hour flight to Fiji didn't leave till 8:00 a.m., but I had to be at the airport two hours ahead of time for the international flight. When I grabbed the travel documents at the office, I noticed that the twenty Gallo Winery employees were mostly interns who had served a year or more with the company.

This trip was to recognize them for their high performance, a nice thing to do, but as the largest winery in the world, Gallo could afford it.

When I arrived at the Air New Zealand ticket counter around 5:45 a.m., the group was already waiting, anxious for the great adventure. Much to my surprise the group was mostly women between the ages of twenty and twenty five along with four men about the same age and two women probably in their early thirties. Apparently, they were not all from Modesto, Gallo's headquarters, but from some offices Gallo had throughout the western states.

Wow! Are these four guys going to have a good time ...and I am going to have a lot of work keeping track of all of them.

As I walked towards the group, two of the young ladies approached me.

"Hi! You must be Jason from the travel agency. I'm

71

Ashlee and this is Corrine," one of them said as they both smiled and held out their hands.

"I am from the agency but Jason couldn't come. I'm Vince Frazier and I'll be taking his place," I returned with a handshake and smile.

At the same time, I heard one of the girls in the group a few feet away say to her friend, "Not a bad switch if you ask me."

Just then the two ladies who appeared to be a few years older than the rest approached with their hands extended.

"Mr. Frazier, I'm Julie White and this is Karen Young. I'm the west coast Director of Interns for Gallo and Karen is my assistant. Glad you could travel with us. I'm sure you have all the tickets and documents we'll need?"

"Nice to meet you," I returned as we shook hands. "I'm pleased to be of service. I do have the tickets and probably need to get to the counter and have all of you checked through."

"Sounds great to me," Julie responded. "We're all excited about Fiji. I don't believe any of us have been there before. Our usual reward trips are to Hawaii."

"Well, you're going to love Fiji. It's incredible! We'll land at the Nadi Airport on the island of Viti Levu. Then we'll take an hour-and-a-half bus ride along the Coral Coast to the Warwick Fiji Resort," I stated loud enough for the whole group to hear."

"I can't wait!" Ashlee said.

"Then please follow me," I said as I walked up to the counter.

When everyone was on the plane, I sat back to catch up on some sleep. Twelve hours was a long time. Fortunately, the man in the seat next to me had already fallen sleep.

I reclined my seat and closed my eyes, but now that I wasn't on task my repressed thoughts kicked in hard. Trisha, Trisha, I kept thinking. How did the ride back go? What did you tell Gary? What are you going to do? How are you feeling about us? Most of all I kept asking myself, what am I going to do about Trisha?

Every time I closed my eyes I could see her delicate features and feel her body pressed against mine. It brought both pleasure and pain, as my heart wasn't sure which emotion to provide.

Chapter Ten

Fiji

After three full length movies, a breakfast, lunch, and dinner, a couple of trips up and down the aisle to check on my travelers, and no sleep, we landed. I felt like I'd been on a Special Forces mission.

The wobbling bus ride along the only and barely-paved road that circled the island of Viti Levu to the Warwick definitely kept me awake.

Upon our arrival I got everyone checked in and placed in their respective rooms. We were just in time for a late dinner.

Now since I was exhausted, I traded dinner for the comfort of my bed and room.

Gallo had provided an all-inclusive experience at the Warwick, so all meals, drinks, non-motorized water craft etc. were included for the group.

About mid-morning, I awoke to some noise outside. As I got up and looked down from my third-floor corner room porch at the beauty of the palm studded beach and the still blue-green waters of the lagoon, I could see three of my young clients already gleefully kayaking by.

My first thought was to admire the energy they had. My second thought was that unlike some of us, they obviously had been able to sleep on the plane.

I was reminded of the elegance and charm of the Warwick as I made my way down the stairs, through the lobby, and down another set of stairs to the ground floor Café Korolevu. It opened to the green grass, flowers, and palm trees that led the way to the white sand beach. I could see the adjoining palm studded island about a hundred feet from the shore that held another resort restaurant, The Wicked Walu.

It was magnificent.

"Mr. Frazier, why don't you join us?" a voice to my left said invitingly.

Julie and Karen were sitting at a table for four sipping coffee.

"Don't mind if I do," I smiled, now ready for some friendly conversation.

"This place is enchanting," Julie said. "I have to commend you and the travel agency."

"Thanks," I returned. "Both would be me since I'm the owner."

"Then how did you end up actually taking a group on a trip?" Julie queried.

"Just plain luck, I guess, along with one of my agents becoming ill at the last moment," I said smiling. "Besides, you can see why I couldn't pass up a chance to return to Fiji, especially since I had a few vacation days left."

"Maybe I'll just stay here and have Gallo send the interns to me," Julie said as she looked out over the still ocean and the canopy of clouds reflected on its surface.

"Hey, not a bad idea. I could set up right next to the tour operators in the front lobby," I stated matter-of-factly as we all laughed.

Karen's laugh was loud, in contrast to her quiet personality, which, along with her brown hair and striking blue eyes, I found attractive.

Julie, on the other hand, in both appearance and personality was in some way even more attractive. Her manner was professional, warm, and intelligent.

Our Fijian waitress came over to assist. She smiled and almost danced as she spoke.

"And what can I get for you this fine morning?"

"I'd just like a coffee refill," Julie stated.

Karen followed her with, "Same for me except I'd like one more of those papaya muffins if you don't mind."

"And you sir, how can I make your morning brighter?" the server asked.

"Coffee sounds great, and I believe I'll take a run through the breakfast buffet."

"Very good. Then I'll bring your coffee and muffin," she said and this time she did appear to actually dance away.

"She seems happy to be working here," Julie observed.

"She probably really is. You'll find the Fijians to be naturally warm and friendly. They still live around the islands in family villages where they share most things. They'll give you a big 'Bula' which is their greeting, kind of like the Hawaiian 'Aloha' followed by a big smile. And they love to have their pictures taken. So don't be shy about asking," I responded.

"Hey Mr. Travel Agent, you've got a lot to share. Makes me think that you've been here before," Julie said smiling.

"Oh, four or five times, but only in my dreams," I said with a chuckle.

Two young women dressed for the beach strolled by.

"Hi Julie, Karen,... and Vince," they said.

"Good morning, Ashlee and Corrine," I returned.

I heard Corrine say quietly to Ashlee, "See, I told you he'd remember our names."

Just then Shawn and Justin, two of the young men from our group, sped by pausing just long enough to smile.

"I wonder where they're going? It sounds like you'd better watch out for those two, Mr. Travel Agent," Julie said as we all laughed again.

After arranging a couple of trips for some of the group to places on the island, I retired down the beach a-ways to get some sun and reading time. On my way I passed Julie, Karen, and a couple of the other young women doing the same near the small island walkway.

Once again, it was Julie who turned my head and caught my eye.

As I walked by with a friendly "Bula," I wondered if having both brains and beauty were qualifications for working at Gallo.

While I sat on the beach with my unread book still in my hand, watching as the tide pulled the water out, I couldn't help but think of Trisha. This was another place on my list I wanted to share with her.

As I thought of her I automatically reached down into my beach bag and pulled out my i-Phone. I clicked it on. There was Trisha in front of Mount Dana with a big smile on her face. In a way she was here with me.

The ocean was breaking over the reef about two hundred yards out and some of the higher old coral reefs were looking like dark heads bobbing up out of the shrinking lagoon. The palms were playing host to a flock of red and green parrots who had just landed noisily above me. I thought if they didn't leave soon, I'd better move over, at least a few feet.

I headed back to my room passing Karen at the outdoor beach shower rinsing off the salt water and sand.

"Hi, Vince, Julie and I were talking and knowing that you're here alone we hoped you'd be able to join us for dinner. We have reservations on the island at The Wicked Walu for 7:00 tonight."

"Good choice for evening dining," I returned. "That sounds like a great idea! I'd be pleased to join you.

Thanks, Karen."

Karen walked off with a smile on her face.

Back in my room I cleaned up and put on a collared shirt with a blue floral design, a pair of khaki slacks, and a light tan jacket.

As I entered The Wicked Walu, I noticed that several members of our group had also made reservations at the island restaurant. I stopped briefly at each table checking on how everyone was doing. Receiving excellent reviews, I moved over to the table for four which stood on a pier over the water.

"You picked the best table in the house."

Julie and Karen were already seated.

"Hi Vince! We're glad you could join us," Julie said, raising her glass of red wine.

"Good evening ladies. You picked the best table in the house. Wait a few minutes until the sun starts to set and nature's entertainment begins."

"Oh," Julie said with a smile, "I thought you were the entertainment, but the sunset will do fine."

"Well the sunset is tough competition so I finally gave up my act and decided to be a travel agent instead," I replied as I sat down.

"And a very good one indeed, if the Warwick is any indication of your abilities," Julie added.

"May I take your order?" the waiter asked.

"Actually, not to be unsophisticated, but I'm really thirsty. You don't happen to have a Harp beer by Guinness do you?" I questioned.

"Yes, we do sir. I'll send someone up to the main restaurant to get one."

"You don't have to do that, Daniel," I replied after noticing his name tag.

"Sir, it's my pleasure," he returned graciously. "And ladies, another glass of Merlot?"

"I'm fine," Karen said

"So am I, thanks Daniel," Julie added.

The sun was starting to drop as it began to place its orange blanket around the evening thunder clouds.

My Harp was in front of me after just a couple of minutes.

"Ladies," I said raising my glass of Harp. "To the wonders of nature, the beauty of Fiji and the enchantment of you two ladies!"

"Thank you, Mr. Frazier," Julie chimed in as all three glasses met.

The sun was beginning to drop.

Since the Wicked Walu specialized in steak and fish, Julie ordered the filet mignon while I ordered the Walu's namesake, the Walu, a white meat fish kind of like Mahi Mahi. Karen who had remained very quiet ordered just a small salad.

"I haven't known you to turn down a great steak before Karen," Julie observed.

"You know, I'm really feeling a little queasy. I think I spent a little too much time in the sun today. I hate to do this but could you please cancel my salad. I think I'll go back to the room and lie down," Karen said with obvious discomfort.

"I have some Alka Seltzer and Pepto-Bismol back in the room if that would help," Julie said.

"Is there anything I can do? I'm sure I have something just for such an emergency in my travel bag," I added.

"Thanks, but I think I just need to get back to the room and rest."

She slowly stood up and headed towards the door.

"I'm sorry we won't have the pleasure of her company," I said to Julie.

"Yeah, me too. She's very seldom ill. I should probably eat and head back to the room to check on her in a little while."

"Sounds like a good plan to me. There's always tomorrow," I stated, trying to be positive with our vanishing evening.

"But we still have the sunset," I added trying to perk both of us up.

Chapter Eleven

A Choice

By now I couldn't tell where the sunset started and the ocean began. There was one brilliant palette of orange, blue, white and grey reflected from the water below us to the highest point in the sky.

Daniel brought our meals and they looked great.

I felt a bit uncomfortable having dinner with another beautiful lady so soon after Trisha had left. As a travel agent I often had meals with clients on trips, but this time it felt rather strange. Julie was a desirable lady and I enjoyed her company, but I felt like I was cheating on my girlfriend. I guess I couldn't get Trisha out of my mind, or didn't want to.

"You know Vince, I really enjoy your company. I find you a bit intriguing, knowledgeable, and capable all at the same time," Julie said as she cut off a piece of fillet.

"Sounds kinda like a boy scout, except missing a couple of merit badges," I returned with a smile. "But thanks. I'm enjoying your company too."

"How long have you had the travel business in Modesto?" Julie asked.

"About ten years. I started it after my B.A., a few years in the service, and my M.B.A. I figured with my desire to travel and my business education, it would be a good fit for me," I replied.

"And has it been?" Julie queried.

"Very much so, but it's kept me from settling down."

"Then you want to settle down and have a family?" she asked.

"Yes, I just need to meet the right person. How about you?" I asked feeling like it was time to switch the questioning around.

"Well yes. My situation is sort of like yours. I did a B.A. in business in San Diego, then took a job as an assistant personal director with the Getty Foundation in Los Angeles. After a few years there I took this job with Gallo and I've been with them ever since," she eagerly replied.

"Then how long have you lived in Modesto?" I asked.

"Well, I'm not in the main office now, I'm in... Is there anything else I can get you?" Daniel asked politely.

"Julie, how about you?" I asked.

"I'm fine and it was excellent," she said.

"I'm through also. The walu was just right, tender and juicy! Thanks Daniel," I added.

"I really need to get back and check on Karen. Why

don't you join us on the beach tomorrow? I'm sure all the young ladies would enjoy that...and I would too."

"Well, I guess I'll see you tomorrow on the beach," I returned as Julie left with a big smile.

I sat still for a moment, taking my last sip of what was now a warm Harp. The sun was down. Only a light blue afterglow reflected off of the still water.

I thought about tomorrow and the beach. I had been working out a bit at a local club. And I did get a good tan in Cancun a couple of weeks ago when I had the misfortune of escorting a large group of graduating high school students for a celebration party. The good news was I was able to get out of there alive after about three days. At least I got a tan, so I should look presentable for the group tomorrow.

I probably sat at the table too long, for my mind again jumped back to Trisha. I wished she had been there with me.

I was up early the next morning as the sun was rising to check on a couple of trips I had scheduled for some of the group. One was an hour and a half bus ride around the island to Suva, the capital of Fiji, for some sightseeing and shopping. The other was a short bus ride and a mile plus hike inland to the Korolevu Falls.

The group to Suva had just left when I headed down to the beach. The white sand sank into the clear blue-green water as the tall palms danced in the wind along the shore as though trying to reach the blue sky above them. It was another gorgeous day in paradise.

"Hi, Vince! Over here," Ashlee yelled.

Of course, she was right in the middle of a small group of interns along with Shawn, Corrine, and Justin.

Julie was on a lounge chair working on her tan while reading a magazine. She was wearing a white two piece suit working on her tan.

"Good article?" I said as I approached.

"Actually, it's the Warwick Resort magazine and I was just reading about Fijian drinks," she answered as she sat up and smiled.

"Did you find out about their traditional 'kava' drink and ceremony?" I inquired.

"Not yet. It's probably on the next page."

"How is Karen doing?" I asked.

"She's still a bit weak, but she'll be all right. I think the combination of too much sun the first day along with two plates of fresh fruit did their job."

"Have a seat," she said as she pointed to the lounge chair next to her.

"How's your morning been? Did you get the Suva group off?" she asked.

"They're on their way. Now to get the falls group going," I added.

"I think that group is down to six, if you're still going that is," Julie mentioned.

"What happened?" I asked curiously.

"This seems to be the day of the week the Warwick has it's volleyball competition and the others wanted to stay and play," she responded.

"We still have a day or so to set up another trip if the rest still want to go," I mentioned.

"I'll check. When do we leave? It looks like it's you, me, Corrine, Ashlee, Justin and Shawn. I think Ashlee's giving up on you," Julie said with a smile.

"It looks like she's switched to Shawn from what I can see," I returned with a chuckle.

"You've got that right," Julie returned, "but then that gives me more time with you."

"Why do I feel like a timeshare?" I said with another chuckle. "And to answer your question, in about an hour."

"Then I'd better get ready. Hey guys we leave for the falls in an hour," she yelled over to the group.

"Be sure to wear your swimwear and tennis shoes or good sandals that you don't mind getting wet. The trail crosses a stream several times," I advised.

An open truck with benches along the sides picked us up and drove inland through the jungle several miles into the mountains. The plant life was everywhere with papayas, mango, mandarin, and bread fruit trees growing just off the dirt road. We came to a small Fijian village and were met by two men. John was to be our trail guide and provided us with long, stout walking poles mostly to help us keep our balance when we crossed the stream. With poles in hand, off we went.

The hike was beautiful, going through various types of jungle canopies, vines, flowers and trees.

The river crossings weren't bad, only one to two feet

deep across ten to fifteen feet of water. The interns hiked anxiously ahead.

"This is fabulous. Just like I imagined," Julie said.

"Paradise in the South Pacific," I returned. "Every time I'm here it's more enchanting."

"Kind of like you, Vince. It sort of grows on you," Julie said softly.

I heard her but decided it was best to just keep on hiking.

"You know, you're the kind of man a girl could become attracted to. Are you available or have you found that 'right person' yet?" Julie asked inquisitively.

"That's a tough one. I thought I had found her, but I just may have lost her. I'm still not certain on that," I said rather cryptically.

"I'm not quite sure what you said, so until you figure it out..." she trailed off as she took my hand.

I did like her. She was the kind of lady I could really be interested in. Again, I got that uncomfortable feeling in my gut. I figured what the heck. It was a beautiful place, I was with a person I considered a friend, so I held on. It was nice.

The Korolevu Falls were perfect. Though they only fell about sixty feet, they were exactly what island falls should be like. Ferns, red hibiscus flowers, and moss grew out along the falls which fell into a deep basin of cool water now full of interns.

Shawn had just climbed up its wall about fifteen feet before throwing himself back in. Ashlee shouted with enthusiasm and applauded.

Julie and I pulled off our hiking shirts and tennis shoes, jumped in, and joined them. Shawn's second cannon ball just missed me. We all splashed around for a while until John told us it was time to hike down and meet the truck.

"How about meeting Karen and me tonight for dinner at the Pappagallo Restaurant," Julie said as we arrived at the hotel.

"Sure! I'd love to! A man has to eat you know," I replied, trying not to be too enthusiastic.

When I returned to my room, I realized I hadn't called the office or talked with Larry since arriving in Fiji. So, I decided to call and bring him up to date on the trip.

"Hey Larry, this is Vince. How are things at home?" I asked. "Everything okay then...Yeah here too. Great trip so far.

"Any important messages? ...None that can't wait, good. ...One strange one for me you couldn't figure out. Who was it from?

"From a woman named Trisha? When she found out I wasn't there she said to tell me what? ...Yeah, I got it, 'Men would fight wars for a night with you! Fight for me.'

"I understand it. Yeah, thanks Larry."

As I hung up the phone a tear came to my eye. Trisha, what am I going to do about you? I stood there for a moment then realized I needed to shower and clean up for dinner. Right now, I needed to move on.

Chapter Twelve

Small World

When I arrived at the Pappagallo restaurant, the Warwick's version of fine Italian-European dining, Julie was already seated at a table without Karen.

Her hair was pulled back. Her black dress looped up over her shoulders and around her neck, with the pearls glowing against her tanned skin.

"You look exceptionally stunning tonight," I said.

"And you're as handsome as always," she returned with a smile.

"I take it Karen isn't coming, or is she going to be late?"

"I'm afraid she has a touch of the flu and is still resting."

"Sorry to hear that. It's really a shame to be here and not be able to enjoy it. Give her my best when you see her," I offered.

"Looks like we're alone again. That's fine with me. I do enjoy your company," I stated as I perused the menu.

"As for me, I could make a habit out of this," Julie said as she looked up from her menu.

The table candles reflected in her eyes giving them an extra sparkle. Her calm and self-assured demeanor was comforting but also made me cautious. This was a lady who was used to being in charge and probably getting what she wanted. Long before now I had figured that I was probably what she wanted.

Although I was flattered and my inner male voice shouted 'go for it,' I still felt the need to put the brakes on.

Just a few days ago I had held Trisha in my arms, and now there was the message left with Larry. Even though I wasn't sure where that was going, I did know that I'd fallen for her and needed to figure it all out. Taking on another relationship, even with a beautiful woman in a South Pacific paradise, put a lot of pressure on my sense of propriety not to mention my heart. I needed to tread lightly.

"I think the fettuccini with the Alfredo sauce sounds delicious to me," I finally said, trying to move the conversation in another direction.

"And that shell fish cannelloni special looks like a treat to me," Julie added.

We both decided to get the house salads. From the wine menu we quickly agreed on an unforgettable New Zealand Sauvignon Blanc from the Highfield Winery that I'd tasted when I was on the southern island a year ago.

"Where do you go next, when you get back to Modesto? What exotic trip is on your calendar?" Julie inquired.

"Being the world traveler that I am, I'll probably spend a lot of time in the office catching up on paper work. Unfortunately, with every pleasure, as you know, there is usually some pain. Although I may take a quick drive to Las Vegas," I stated.

Julies eyes got bigger and a broad smile appeared on her face.

"That's where my office is now!" she said excitedly.

"I thought you worked for Gallo in Modesto?"

"I didn't get a chance to tell you. I had worked in Modesto but I was transferred to their offices in Las Vegas a few years ago," she replied.

"Gallo has a major office in Las Vegas?" I asked a bit surprised.

"Just how many truckloads of wine and beverages do you think they have to ship and distribute in that town each day?" Julie returned with a little laugh.

"Looking at it from that perspective it's probably a ten-story building."

We both laughed.

"Maybe we could get together. I could show you the town," she said with enthusiasm.

"That's a possibility, but I'll be there on personal business."

"Then if that's a maybe I'll take it," she said as she smiled and took a sip of the Sauvignon Blanc that now filled our glasses in front of us.

It was another excellent meal, as usual, up to the high standards of the Warwick.

I'd enjoyed the conversation and companionship.

We wandered out a few feet across the lawn that sloped down to the lagoon beach.

As we walked along the surf, after dropping our sandals on a beach chair, we could feel the light evening breeze blowing across our faces and the warm Fijian ocean on our feet.

"To me, only a few places in the world can match it," I said as I felt her take my hand.

At first, I was a little startled, but we'd held hands before as we hiked to the falls, so why not.

It was a cloudless night, unusual for the South Pacific with its characteristic late afternoon thunderstorms. Both the stars and half crescent moon were glimmering over the ocean above us.

"If I could only wear stars like diamonds," Julie said blissfully looking up into the sky.

Although I kept walking my heart began to race. Did I hear her right? I tried hard to remain calm.

"That's a lovely saying. Where did it come from?" I asked checking to see if I'd really heard her right.

"Oh, I heard my roommate at San Diego State University use it years ago," she returned.

I stopped walking, dropped Julie's hand and turned to look at her. She looked a bit confused.

"It means that..." she started to say.

"If you could wear the stars, they would not only look beautiful, but you could pull one off your necklace and make a wish whenever you wanted," I interrupted her.

I could see Julie's startled look.

"You're right. How in the world did you know that?"

I felt like I'd been hit with a fifty-foot wave. My mind ran an instant replay, Julie, Las Vegas, San Diego State, Maid of Honor...Trisha I thought, as I tried to gain my composure.

"You don't happen to have a friend named Trisha Keys?"

With that, Julie flinched, and her mouth dropped open.

"Yes...I do...She's my best friend...How do you know that?"

"I met her recently," I returned.

"At Lee Vining?" she quickly asked.

"Yes," was all I was able to get out.

"Then you're the one she told me about just as I was leaving for San Francisco when she returned with Gary to Las Vegas?" she said in amazement.

"Probably. We had become rather close in a very short time," I uttered.

"Wow, you can say that again! When she got back, we only had a little time together before I had to leave. Gary tore off quite upset. Trisha was in tears when she told me not to worry anymore about a wedding. I wasn't sure what happened," she said nervously.

"Then she's all right?" I asked concerned.

"I'm not sure how she is. I do know that she was going to call off the engagement with Gary and she hoped to tell him on their trip to Lee Vining, so the wedding thing didn't surprise me. I also figured she was upset when Gary didn't show up because of me. I was tossed out of my apartment at the last minute because the landlord was having the building tented due to a termite infestation. Gary stayed to help me move," she explained.

All I could seem to do was listen, even though a hundred questions cluttered my mind. By now we found ourselves sitting on the sand. It was like all the wind had just been sucked out of us, and like a balloon, we had deflated on that spot.

"What else did she tell you?" I finally asked.

"Well," she began, her composure starting to return, "that she'd met a man, and fallen in love with him in two days. That no one had ever made her feel that way before. Because of the situation with Gary and not being totally open with you about him, she felt she had probably lost you."

My finger made a series of circles in the sand.

"It's amazing," I said. "Life is like a circle. It keeps spinning around in a world that's really so small. Julie, thanks for sharing that with me."

"I wouldn't have said so much, but right now her friendship overshadows my feelings for you, Vince. As Trisha's friend, knowing how she feels about you, I needed to tell you," Julie said quietly.

With that, I took her hand and held it as we both looked out over the ocean.

The low tide had produced pieces of the old dark coral, illuminated by the resort's torches that were burning along the shore.

"Vince," Julie said softly, "what are you going to do?"

"She's the reason I've not opened up to you. She's always on my mind. I trusted her...I'm not sure Julie, I'm not sure," was all I could say.

I had trouble sleeping that night. What should I do? I hadn't felt like calling her when I got back to Modesto. I was racing to get to San Francisco and get the Gallo group settled at the Warwick. When I finally had a little time to think last night, I checked for the paper Trisha had given me at Tuolumne Meadows with her phone number on it and realized it was at home, still in the pocket of the coat I'd been wearing at the time. I could get it from Julie, but did I really want to call?

I went down to an early breakfast at the Café Korolevu. To my surprise Julie was sitting alone at a table at the far end of the eating area.

"Do you mind if I join you?" I asked.

"Please do. I am expecting Karen in a while."

"Then she's feeling better?" I asked.

"Much better," was her reply.

We sat for a moment as the waitress placed a cup of coffee in front of me and refilled Julie's.

"You know this is hard on me too," she said. "I was falling for someone who turned out to be a guy, who my best friend had just fallen for... Go figure."

"If it wasn't for Trisha, any other time or place you would have had my complete attention, and more. You're a talented and beautiful lady," I added, meaning what I said.

"Thanks Vince. Why do you have to be so nice? It makes it harder. Knowing you may end up with my best friend does help a bit. You are going to, aren't you?"

"I had checked to see if I could get an early flight out and maybe return by Sunday, west coast time, since I'll gain a day. There is one I can catch. I could then either fly to Las Vegas on Monday or drive the nine hours down. So, you can see I'm giving it serious consideration," I stated.

"You probably know that if you don't have her phone number I do, Vince."

"Yes, thank you. If I talk to her it needs to be in person. Only then will I be able to evaluate my true feelings," I stated figuring I could be open with Julie.

"You know Vince, it took all of my professional power last night not to call her. I've not talked to her since I left and I've been worried. She's a strong person but this has really thrown her," Julie shared.

"If I left on Sunday could you get the group back okay in a few days? It should be all arranged."

"Sure, Vince. I'd be happy to. I took a count this morning and I think we still have all the interns with us.

Besides, I think you need to go. And I hate to say it, but I think you have to go."

"Thanks a lot, Julie. I'll check on the flight," I returned.

"What flight?" Karen asked as she walked up.

"Good to see you up, Karen. Sorry I have to go, but I'm sure Julie will be more than happy to fill you in. Besides I have the feeling that you girls will be talking about it anyway, so...enjoy the rest of your stay," I said as I worked my way back to my room.

I got the flight I wanted, so I took the hour and half bus ride around the island to the Nadi Airport. I knew Julie had been right. I had to go. At last both my head and my heart were working together.

Chapter Thirteen

Where We Left Off

The twelve-hour flight seemed to take forever. I never had enjoyed the many long flights I'd been on. However, this time I found that I was able to sleep a good part of the trip. That hadn't happened before. Maybe it was because I'd finally figured out what I wanted in life which gave me some peace of mind. I only had to watch two movies before we landed on Sunday at 2:00 p.m. in San Francisco.

I quickly went to get my baggage and then go through customs. I knew the traffic in the Bay Area would be light Sunday early afternoon, but I was still in a hurry to take the hour and a half plus drive back to Modesto.

I breezed through customs and out the door.

"Vince! Vince!"

Startled, I turned around. It was Trisha! She ran over to me as I dropped my bags. Within a moment she was nestled in my arms. Tears were running down her face. They were also running down mine.

We kissed. We cried. It was as if we had never been apart! At the same time, it seemed we'd been separated for years. I knew I'd made the right choice even before we spoke.

"Trisha, how'd you know I'd be...Julie!"

I should have known, best friends and all as Trisha nodded in between more kisses.

"Vince, Gary's gone! I just want to be with you. These last few days have been miserable for me. I know we're meant to be together," Trisha half cried.

"Trisha, I know that now too. I couldn't stop thinking about you!" I said as I returned her kiss.

"Vince, I called and tried to tell you what happened. I wanted you to know everything."

"I know, Trisha. I just found out about your call on Saturday. Larry gave me the message and I knew that I would...."

"Would what, Vince?"

"Fight a war for another night with you," I whispered into her ear.

I took her hand as we slowly walked towards the parking area. We couldn't help but stop now and then for a quick hug or kiss. I was overwhelmed. I knew I wanted her, but where would we go from here? How were we going to work out being together when she was in Las Vegas and I in Modesto?

"Vince, when I heard from Julie, she said some very nice things about you. When she told me you were coming back from Fiji early to find me, I couldn't help myself. I knew I had to drive all night and be here. I wanted to be with you, hoping you were sure you wanted to be with me. I had to know."

"And what did you find out?" I smiled and asked.

"That you want me too! That you want to give our love a chance to grow even more," Trisha said, her light blue eyes looking into mine as she turned me around for another kiss.

"Trisha, there is so much I want to tell you, so much I still want to share."

"We have some time Vince. I was able to arrange for several days off from the hospital. We can be together. We can build from where we left off."

I knew what I needed to do, what I wanted to do.

"Trisha, did you drive your Audi here?"

"Yes, Vince. I have it back now."

"I want you to follow me back to my place in Modesto. Do you have a Maps application in your car," I asked.

"Yes, I do," Trisha said.

"You may want to save that line, for later," I said with a big smile and laugh, at which point I received another big hug and kiss.

"We'll program it to my address in case we get separated," I suggested.

The Bay Area traffic was light but the trip back seemed to take as long as my flight from Fiji. Heading east on the 580 near Livermore we hit some traffic and got separated. I knew Trisha had the directions programmed in so she'd be all right.

When I turned into my driveway in the Dutch Hollow area of northwest Modesto, I didn't see Trisha, but I knew she'd be along.

I ran inside, quickly changed, and grabbed some things and threw them into my Highlander just as Trisha pulled up.

"You have a beautiful home Vince, is it country French style?" she asked.

"Yes, I had it built, but right now I want to take you somewhere. We'll have time later to spend here. Will you come with me?" I asked.

"Vince, I'd go anywhere with you."

"It's a bit of a drive. Do you need to step in for a moment?" I asked.

"I'm fine Vince, always fine when I'm with you," she said as I received another kiss.

We both climbed into my Highlander and took off. Trisha had this curious look in her eyes but decided not to ask.

We headed east up Highway 120. We stopped for dinner at the quaint little 49'er gold mining town of Groveland. I'd made reservations for a nice dinner at the Groveland Hotel.

"Is this where we're going?" Trisha asked curiously as we both started on some salmon fillets. "It's beautiful, I've never been in this area before."

"This is part of it, Trisha."

After finishing an incredible dinner, we headed

back to the Highlander.

Darkness had fallen quickly and besides the outline of the road and trees, little could be seen. It seemed like we were in a capsule together in dark space, floating to our final destination. And that was fine with both of us. We talked about everything, including Julie, Gary, my trip to Fiji, and what we liked about each other.

Almost before either of us knew it, I was braking and turning down a narrow road lined with trees.

We pulled up into a parking spot with our headlights hitting a large green container. Julie leaned forward staring at it for a moment. Then a big simile spread across her face as it did mine.

"Are we ...at the Lodge?" she asked.

"Well you said we could be together and build from where we left off," I answered.

As we got out of the car, I handed Trisha the largest flashlight, held her hand tightly, and pulled her close to me as we headed toward the registration building.

"I want you close in case we come across a bear."

The lights were still on as the last few diners were finishing their meals.

As we peeked in, I spotted Danny behind the counter. He smiled waved and put his thumb up. I thought, thank goodness for cell phones.

"What now?" Trisha asked as I led her up the hill.

After a few more steps we could see a glowing light just front of us. The Dana Fork was rushing by to our right as we heard the mournful sound of the waterfall

We could see a glowing light in front of us.

in the distance.

"Lady Trisha, may I present to you Cabin 10," I said pulling open the screen door.

Several candles lit the room. The two single cots were gone. Only the double remained. The card table was covered with a white table cloth, napkins, silverware, two wine glasses, and plates. On a small table next to one of the chairs a bottle of wine, a plate of mixed fruit and nuts, another of cheese and crackers, and two smaller plates each holding chocolate mousse.

"How'd you ever get all this..." Trisha started to say.

"Magic...a cell phone... and a friend," I smiled.

Trisha reached over and pulled me to her. Her arms were tight around me as mine were around her. Our kiss was the one we'd both been waiting for, one that neither of us would ever forget.

"Trisha."

"Yes, my love."

"We'll need to eat soon. It's getting late and colder, and we'll need to clean up before we hop in bed," I said.

"Then you can't wait to get in bed, warm up, and finish what we started the last time we were here?" Trisha said slowly and quietly.

"Oh, yes, that too. No, I was concerned about cleaning up all this food before the bears arrived," I said with a big smile.

At which point I received a quick punch on my shoulder.